METAL

HARD TIME, BOOK 1

EREC STEBBINS

TWICE PI PRESS

Only one thing is impossible for God: to find any sense in any copyright law on the planet.—Mark Twain

Hard Time, Book 1: Metal. Copyright © 2018 Erec Stebbins

Published 2018 by Twice Pi Press, erecstebbinsbooks.com

Cover design by Erec Stebbins © 2018. Edited by Michael Matheson.

ePub ISBN-13: 978-1-942360-34-6

Kindle ISBN-13: 978-1-942360-35-3

Paperback ISBN-13: 978-1-942360-36-0

Content Guide

This novel contains depictions and references to events and ideas that some will find disturbing, possibly including, but not limited to, monsters, gore, death, torture, captivity, severe illness, pain, fear, medical procedures, and violence. There is also profanity and strong language, the challenging of some accepted norms, and the questioning of different kinds of authority, religious and secular. The book may also contain religion, Oxford commas, and an unnecessary number of tpyos and, grammer misteaks. Readers are asked to prepare accordingly.

1

SELF

2

93 Post Singularity

AI VIDEO/AUDIO TRANSCRIPT
AUTONOMOUS SURVEILLANCE WITNESS X949Q34
PAN AMERICAN COMMUNITY COURT OF APPEALS
ENGLISH TRANSLATION
RECORDING COMMENCED ON ENTRY OF JUDGE
RAPHAELA LOPEZ, 10:03, 3RD OF APRIL

[*A side door opens and the Judge enters the court chambers.*]

BAILIFF: All rise.

JUDGE LOPEZ: You may be seated. First order of business is the late motion by the prosecution to render authority from PAC to the Autonomous State of Texas and Greater Oklahoma. Motion has been considered and is denied. The Court concedes that Maria Pérez served as part of the Texas army in the Unified American Deployment. However, defendant's crimes were alleged across a clear zone of PAC jurisdiction. [Inaudible] Attorneys will now present their closing statements.

MR. GARCIA: Your honor, esteemed jurors, PAC Enforcement Officers, fellow citizens—I won't waste your time. The facts in this case have been presented. A preponderance of independently verified, multi-perspective drone video footage and audio. Video and audio from the Infantry Mech of Sergeant Pérez herself. Sworn testimony of twenty-three eyewitnesses from average citizens to other soldiers on duty. There is no challenge to the clear narrative, absolutely no doubt about what transpired that day.

[*Prosecuting attorney Garcia leaves his desk and approaches the juror box.*]

MR. GARCIA: In an act of pre-meditated murder, Mech Sergeant Maria Pérez, in full battle armor and weaponry, marched on the seaport village of Acajutla in El Salvador. There, she trained her guns on the protesting civilians exercising their Article 7 rights. She viciously slaughtered three hundred and forty of them in cold blood.

[*Shouts erupt from the court audience.*]

JUDGE LOPEZ: We've had enough of that! Any more outbursts will be met with immediate arrest and removal from the court!

MR. GARCIA: As we can see, the people want justice. And justice must be rendered for these crimes. Sergeant Pérez was an officer of the PAC. She's sworn to protect and defend the citizens therein, even those challenging the actions of the government. But this daughter of a former disgraced General, a father who led a failed coup and spent his last hours behind bars, had other ideas. The rage against democratic norms led her to disregard the law and the rights of the people. Led her to ignore the direct orders of her superiors to stand down. As the recordings show, even as they shouted over her coms, she shut them down. She avenged her father to restore the family honor. She took it upon herself to enact a retribution against innocents the likes of which we have never seen. She violated the code and oath of the Mechanized Infantry. She disgraced herself and her family. And you, as the jury, have the opportunity to right that wrong, to repay injustice with justice.

[*Mr. Garcia walks between the jury box and the table for the defense.*]

MR. GARCIA: Some will find any means to turn your eyes from these unspeakable horrors. Some will seek sympathy from you for the accused. They will explain away this slaughter as madness, as the fault of others, as technology gone wrong.

[*Mr. Garcia turns and places his hands on the edge of the jury box.*]

MR. GARCIA: Don't let them. Don't let them distract you with half-baked theories of doctors and therapists. Our caregivers always see the best in people, and thank goodness for that. But a doctor isn't a judge. A therapist isn't an officer of the law. And thank goodness for that! Or there would be no justice. Without laws, without responsibility, all the empathy in the world won't save civilization from the lawless. Maria Pérez committed monstrous crimes and betrayed the public trust. You can hold her accountable. I believe and trust in your honor to do what is right. Find her *guilty*. Thank you.

JUDGE LOPEZ: Mr. Sanchez, your closing statement?

[*Mr. Sanchez stands and gestures toward his client.*]

MR. SANCHEZ: The prosecutor is right about one thing: we aren't here to contest the events of that day. But we are most certainly here to contest this witch hunt! One that has excused reckless and monstrous actions of the PAC military. One that scapegoats their crimes with my client. The Mechanized Infantry was formed decades ago. It took place over the concerns and protests of citizens like those killed in Acajutla. That's because the PAC military crossed the line from defense to madness. We *all* know the story. The brain implants. The cocktails of stimulants and aggression hormones. The virtual simulations that led to an entire generation of soldiers locked away in institutions. Their brains fried. Their families devastated. Many of you know. Many have a friend or relative still suffering from the damage of those early years.

[*Mr. Sanchez approaches the jury.*]

MR. SANCHEZ: But now we are to believe all is well with their Frankenstein soldier program. Now we are to trust that this reckless and unstable technology is free of danger. We are to ignore the incidents that continue to give lie to this claim. We are to believe that a model soldier, a mother of three and loving wife, secretly nursed hatred for the punishment of her family's crimes. Medical experts tell us that the Mech program is equivalent to prolonged brain trauma. So we're supposed to treat these soldiers as ordinary men and women? Are they free like you and me to make proper choices between right and wrong? Are the brain damaged victims of the military fully able to judge when actions become crimes? Sergeant Pérez is as much a victim of PAC warmongering as the innocents that found their way on the wrong end of a terrible technology. Chemicals and electricity were pumped into her brain. All designed to make soldiers into killing machines at one with their mech. And they turned a good woman, a good soldier, into a madwoman one October evening.

[*Mr. Sanchez steps backward to stand beside his client.*]

MR. SANCHEZ: You can follow the letter of the law and the shouts for blood from the understandably bereaved. But it won't be justice, it'll be a mockery. The prosecutor is right that someone should pay for what has happened. But my client is the wrong person for you to set your sights on. She is a tool. A damaged and traumatized tool of far guiltier parties who hide in the shadows. Who continue to operate with impunity. Convicting my client will let them know that it's okay to use humans as fodder for their war machine. That innocent civilians are expendable collateral damage. That in the end, no one will ever hold them accountable. But you can send a different message. You can show that the world sees through the facade of the technological powers. You can render a verdict of *not guilty* by reason of insanity. It's the *right* verdict. It will give Maria Pérez a chance to heal. To seek treatment for what *they* have done to her. It will send a message to the powers who are *truly* responsible for this. And if that happens, you would be the force that helps prevent future atrocity. *That* would be justice. Thank you.

[*Mr. Sanchez sits down beside his client and speaks with her softly. Their words are audible only to the ASW microphones.*]

MS. PEREZ: Thank you, Xico.

[*Judge Lopez speaks to the jury.*]

JUDGE LOPEZ: You have now heard the final statements. As discussed, deliberations will begin today and continue until a verdict is reached.

MR. SANCHEZ: I don't know if it's going to be enough, Maria. [Inaudible]

MS. PEREZ: It doesn't matter. Doesn't matter what they decide or call me here or on the streets. I know who I am.

2

NONSELF

I don't know who I am.

She shivered. Sweat beaded and poured down her eyes. A disorienting loss of personhood churned inside, gusts of panic blocking out the horror around her.

The endless desert vanished. The river of bones gone. For a frozen moment, she forgot even the blistering, bloody swollen star and its violation of the sky.

I don't know my name. I don't know where I am. I don't know who I am.

She gaped at the interior. A dizzying mess of projected 3D screens and position-sensitive controls, voice-activation, struggling climate control and radiation shielding surrounded her. Bulging cannons outside the thick window jutted from the sides.

I'm in a mech.

That she *knew* it was a mech—a battle optimized survival chassis—that it stood like some lonely toy soldier in the middle of hell, that a few moments of examination made it clear she could in fact *operate* it, all made as much sense as the fact that she had no idea why she could. Or why she was in the damn thing to begin with.

A journey?

There was some journey she was supposed to make. A long and dangerous journey.

Why?

Impossible. Fogged thoughts danced in her mind but wouldn't solidify, couldn't be grasped and tamed and examined. Someday she might remember, leash the fleeting dreams to reality. But it mattered little now. *Now*, she had to move. Or she'd die.

The woman's arms raised and danced through space, tapping projected screens. Climate came first. She studied the environmental readouts and grimaced. An absurd amount of radiation flooded her mech.

Her mech?

Yes. *Her* mech.

Her mech baked in a planetary oven. Not so absurd

considering the monster star hanging over her like some dripping orb of lava. But the quantity of energy assaulting the landscape maxed out the design specs. Despite the thick, metal walls of the battle armor, radiation flooded the cockpit. Her dosage peaked in the red, her caramel skin darkening with a hint of burgundy. Wavelength sensors blinked warnings.

I'm getting cooked to death.

The heat crushed her. Despite the mech working overtime to cool the air, the system was failing. The inside temperature crept toward feverish. Sweat pooled on the floorboard. The temperature of the machinery rose without pause. At this rate she might overheat the mech in hours.

I've got to cut power, reduce function.

Choices had to be made. The wrong ones meant death.

Maybe all of them will kill me. Maybe that's why I'm here. To die.

She shook her head, snapping her thoughts to the machine. She swiped to reduce climate control. She shut down the rocketry, cooling down the vertical blasters. It made her more vulnerable, taking away an easy escape route. But it reduced the strain on the mech. She went through a list of functions from communications to emergency systems and shut them all down.

The temperature increase slowed, but continued. She'd bought time. Could the mech hold together until that bright fire plunged below the horizon?

Please let this hateful desert cool down at night.

Expanding the fuel cell and battery window, she laughed. Power wasn't going to be an issue. She even dialed up the screening on the solar cells to reduce input by ninety percent. This sandpit didn't lack for light.

Navigation was useless. No satellite communication, no integrated GPS for the AI. Just a magnetic field and direction. She shut it all down and decided to rely on more primitive tools.

Bones.

The bones alone broke the terrible symmetry of the sands. The trail of bones cut the space from horizon to horizon in half. As far as the telescopic sight of the mech could see, it didn't falter. And it thickened in one direction, the density of the pink ceramic growing. Another symmetry broken.

Go where the bones grow.

Madness. A plan untethered to reason. But with so little to cling to—with no memories, no sense of place, no companionship—that river of skeletons held tangible reality in this lair of insanity. The bones and that lurking red reaper above.

She would follow the road of bones. Living things had been here. Their remains were still exposed in the sands.

Living things that died on this poisoned path. Hundreds. Thousands. Tens of thousands of doomed creatures.

Madness.

Massive holes slunk in the depths of her mind. She accepted that awful reality, couldn't turn away from the truth that she was broken and ill. But whatever had happened, however damaged her mind, however much hope she summoned *ex nihilo* to grasp a lifeline in this land of extinction, a dread certainty ate through her thoughts.

She stared at the bones until the pink line met the horizon. She knew that her skeleton would soon be joining them.

Giving the universe the finger through her window, she cursed and grabbed the virtual controls, waving her arms through the air. Her feet jogged in an elliptical arc on the rider.

Stomach juices surged as the mech moved. The giant lumbered forward, sand flying and bones crunching underneath the broad footpads.

2 **93 Post Singularity**

AUDIO TRANSCRIPT

AUTONOMOUS SURVEILLANCE WITNESS XW45T9-78

PAN AMERICAN COMMUNITY FORCE

ENGLISH TRANSLATION

RECORDING COMMENCED ON EXIT OF DEFENDANT

AND COUNSEL FROM THE COURTROOM

16:03, 3RD OF APRIL

[*Convicted murderer Maria Pérez is held in field restraints and escorted by autonomous security forces from the courtroom to her holding cell. Her legal counsel accompanies her.*]

MS. PEREZ: Do these damned bugs have to buzz around us constantly?

MR. SANCHEZ: Bugs? Oh. PAC directives are for all law-enforcement related matters to be documented. I'm afraid they aren't going away, Maria.

MS. PEREZ: I can't walk straight! These electric cuffs and those damn flying cameras spinning around. It's noon and the damn street lights are on!

MR. SANCHEZ: There was another nanoparticle release from the orbital climate sats while you've been in holding. It's kicking in with the light this week. Going to have a short summer.

MS. PEREZ: Well, I'm going to slip on this solar walkway and fall on my face. Great design. Solar paneled everything and then they decide to dim the sun.

MR. SANCHEZ: It's the only way to cool the planet until the CO_2 is sponged out. You know that.

MS. PEREZ: Never paid much attention in school. Kicked the mech-sims asses. ROTC was packed with scouts. Who needs class? God. Today was awful. Did they have to parade me through the street like that? Wouldn't some armored hovercraft have done to zip me from court?

MR. SANCHEZ: They had some angry mobs to feed. Look, we're nearly there. I'd like to go to one of the conference rooms when we arrive. So we can talk.

MS. PEREZ: What's there to talk about? I killed kids and moms and dads. I'm going to be vaporized. Suppose I have it coming.

MR. SANCHEZ: Yes. Well. There are ways to judge that.

MS. PEREZ: Just one judge in the room, though, huh? Jury wasn't going to turn a mass murderer loose. Judge will hand me my ass, don't worry. *Jesus.* You know, it was like a dream. That whole nightmare. I swear the injection mixture was off. I never reacted to the hits like that before. Doesn't matter.

MR. SANCHEZ: Other things might matter. Just let me explain in a different setting. And maybe we'll meet someone.

MS. PEREZ: Meet someone? Who? Why?

MR. SANCHEZ: Trust me.

[*Pérez and Sanchez enter the maximum security detention structure ZF-3. Following ID clearance and continued PAC Force escort, they obtain permission to use counsel conference room ZF-3.M433.04. They sit across from each other at a rectangular table.*]

MR. SANCHEZ: Your case presents difficult choices to the PAC brass.

MS. PEREZ: Yeah, torching me must be really hard on them.

MR. SANCHEZ: Maria, hear me out. There's serious politics involved. It's an election year. The usual forces are lining up. The Green Left is set to take control of parliament from Secure PAC. But you've muddied the waters. Your case has people divided up in confusing ways about the verdict.

MS. PEREZ: About killing me, you mean.

MR. SANCHEZ: The law is clear. You have to die. We've discussed this. I fought hard to get you off. You were wronged, whatever guilt you carry. But if they execute you, it's going to energize the Green Left. Secure PAC knows they could be swept out of power for it. Judge Lopez is a conservative appointee, but she's street smart. She doesn't want to hand down a verdict that will destroy her party.

MS. PEREZ: I'd laugh if it weren't my head on the block.

MR. SANCHEZ: It doesn't have to be.

MS. PEREZ: My head? You just said—

MR. SANCHEZ: What if I told you that there's another option? A way out for you and a way out for the powers that be. A way for them to look tough on your crimes but technically escape capital punishment.

MS. PEREZ: Life?

MR. SANCHEZ: Legally they can't. Not for your crimes.

MS. PEREZ: Then what?

MR. SANCHEZ: I told you there's someone I wanted you to meet. I'd like to bring her in and introduce you.

MS. PEREZ: Yeah. Okay.

[Mr. *Sanchez exists room ZF-3.M433.04 and returns with a middle-aged woman. Facial scan analysis identifies her as Doctor Taga Lerner, records match as a lead scientist at the EON Corporation. They both sit across from Ms. Pérez.*]

DR. LERNER: Hello, Ms. Pérez. You'll have to excuse me, my Spanish is poor. I was educated in the Asian Alliance and focused my schooling on Mandarin.

MS. PEREZ: Bad Spanish. Good Mandarin. Four-lens smart contacts scanning me now or I ain't seen nothing. Who's the geek, Xico?

MR. SANCHEZ: Maria, this is Taga Lerner. She's a scientist.

MS. PEREZ: Oh. Well. A scientist. So, doc, hear you've got a proposition.

DR. LERNER: Have you heard of the Exile Project?

MS. PEREZ: Ha! Some sort of bullshit teleporter? Crazy ass idea to send convicts to the moon or something?

DR. LERNER: Not a teleporter. Not exactly. And not the moon. But the Exile Project is about sending you somewhere, far away, where you can't hurt anyone here, ever again.

MS. PEREZ: It's real?

DR. LERNER: Very much.

MS. PEREZ: Okay, Xico, you're just fucking with me, now. Get her out of here.

DR. LERNER: We're not! I've been involved with the development of this technology since I was a graduate student in Beijing. The Exile Project is a specific adaptation. Very popular in China when proposed for handling hardened criminals and political activists.

MS. PEREZ: So, you have some super-prison somewhere? Antarctica? In orbit? Zap us there?

DR. LERNER: I'm not at liberty to discuss the details.

MS. PEREZ: Can't tell me where you're going to zap or rocket me? Fuck that. Xico, I'm out.

[Ms. Pérez stands on her side of the table. Mr. Sanchez mirrors the action, holding his palms toward her.]

MR. SANCHEZ: Maria, wait!

MS. PEREZ: Are you shitting me? The jury just condemned my ass. The judge is going to sentence me next week. My life is over. You bring in this beaker bimbo to talk about some fucking trip to who knows where? Are you kidding me?

DR. LERNER: You can mock me all you want, Ms. Pérez. But as you note, you are out of options. You'll be sentenced to die.

MS. PEREZ: I will! And your bullshit magic door ain't gonna change that!

MR. SANCHEZ: Maria, look. Just sit.

[*Ms. Pérez glares at the two people in front of her and then takes her seat.*]

MR. SANCHEZ: It sounds crazy. I know. But back-channel discussions with a lot of powerful people—

people interested in averting an election year scandal —have floated the idea. This Exile Project—they're selling it around the world now. Important people have seen demonstrations. It's been tested. Things...*travel*. It's catching on more and more. The judge is sympathetic to the idea. There are some loopholes in the law.

MS. PEREZ: They want me dead. Touring the asteroids or whatever ain't dead.

DR. LERNER: It might depend on the destination and definitions. It can be argued that certain displacements are legally equivalent to death.

MS. PEREZ: Legally equivalent to death. So am I going to be dead or not?

DR. LERNER: That's my point. It's hard to know.

MS. PEREZ: Mother Mary.

DR. LERNER: We've worked with governments the world over. We've identified a destination. It's both reachable with current tech and significantly blurs the definitions of many capital punishment statutes. We can hand the authorities the technology for a sentence that's harsh and yet obviously not exactly an execution.

MS. PEREZ: Not following.

DR. LERNER: We've spent years calculating a destination. One that is harsh, a hell on Earth. One where you'll very likely suffer and die. But it's not certain. Supplies, items for survival, will be provided. As the Exile Project is used in more and more places, as more and more convicts are transported, you may also have a community to work together.

MS. PEREZ: A community of murderers, sadists, rapists, gang-bangers, and your odd fucking psychopath. So, how do you do this? What happens to me?

DR. LERNER: There's a facility. Its location is a guarded secret just like the destination. There are certain technical difficulties in assuring that you can arrive without instant death.

MS. PEREZ: This is nuts. How is this possible?

DR. LERNER: A point motion is possible for which the four-dimensional path is effectively a closed one. In this case one and the same material point can be present in an arbitrarily small space-time region in several seemingly mutually independent exemplars.

MS. PEREZ: Fuck that. What's that mean?

DR. LERNER: We can rig the distortion of space and time to get you to a highly specific place. Where you are no longer a threat to society. You get another chance to reform your ways.

MS. PEREZ: Nobody will believe this crap.

MR. SANCHEZ: They have, Maria. I told you. They've seen tests. The politicians loved it. Prosecutors ate it up. Solves a lot of problems. Less money for jails. No body bags for the bleeding hearts to go on hunger strikes about. Out of sight, out of political trouble.

MS. PEREZ: Might land me in a mountain or ocean or something.

DR. LERNER: It's new tech. No promises, even if we have some countermeasures to protect the initial transfer. The tests we can make have worked well. But we can't check the final destination. It's a one-way ticket. On purpose.

MS. PEREZ: You're likely just firing us into the sun.

DR. LERNER: The coordinates have been verified by scientists in the international community. It should work. But your other option is certain death. So the question is, do you want to fight for more life later, or just end it now?

MS. PEREZ: One condition. My mech goes with me.

DR. LERNER: I don't think—

MS. PEREZ: Non-negotiable. You want me to guinea pig for your mad scientist machine. Make the money men and politicians happy. Well, then, my mech goes. Gives me a leg up in the apocalypse. *Come on.* Should be an easy sell. Get rid of the she-devil *and* her monster.

MR. SANCHEZ: They might indeed like that.

DR. LERNER: All right, Ms. Pérez. I'll see what I can do.

4

***

SENTENCE

2 93 Post Singularity

Audio Transcript
Autonomous Surveillance Witness M47-009598
Pan American Community Court of Appeals
English Translation
final courtroom recording
10:28, 10th of June

[Convicted murderer Maria Pérez continues her silence during the victim impact testimony of ten speakers who have lost family members during her attack on the protesting crowds of Acajutla.]

JUDGE LOPEZ: And we will hear our final statement. Mr. Branco, would you please take the stand? [Inaudible.] Thank you. You have five minutes.

MR. BRANCO: Hello. My name is Enrique Santos Aresta Branco. I am a dockworker. October 14 I lost my entire family. My wife, Violetta. My two grown daughters, Maria and Sophia. My little boy, Ricardo. In a moment, they were gone. Everything in my mind, my soul. Gone. Just like that. Forever. They weren't protesting. My son was sick! I was working. Violetta asked our daughters help her bring little Richi to the physician. She'd heard the protests had come to our sector. But she had to go. Even if there was violence, it was always in the front. Contained. It should've been safe.

[Mr. Branco points a trembling arm toward Ms. Pérez.]

MR. BRANCO: Except for her. In that devil machine. There was no safe place! Armored rounds the size of my arm. Missiles and grenades. Burning chemicals. When we went to search for our families, it broke us. Hell itself couldn't be worse. It can't be described. I never found their bodies. So little remained of any bodies. Too many body parts and lakes of blood. Somewhere in Acajutla whatever was left of my little ones, my beautiful wife, everything was tossed into great pits. Chemicals thrown over to cover the rotting. Men in blood-splattered plastic suits swimming through a pond of meat. *Like a stew.* Now I have nothing. And I want just one thing. Destroy this she-devil. Kill it. Purge the world of every last piece of its evil. It's not hate. I can't feel hate anymore. The death of this devil won't give me peace. But it will take away one part of the fire inside. Because I see a monster lurking among us. A monster ready to slaughter the innocent again. *Please.* I beg you. *Destroy* it.

[Mr. Branco stands and glares at Ms. Pérez. He turns to Judge Lopez and exits the witness box, leaving the courtroom.]

JUDGE LOPEZ: We have heard from all sides now. Normally, I'd adjourn to assess everything before sentencing, but civil unrest forces my hand. Justice must be rendered today, before more violence and injustice consume our lands. The convicted will please rise for sentencing.

[Ms. Pérez and her attorney rise.]

JUDGE LOPEZ: Maria Pérez, you have been convicted of heinous crimes against humanity, murder, and the violation of your PAC oath. In accordance with numerous statutes outlined in previous sessions, I have no choice but to sentence you to death.

[The courtroom fills with cheers and applause. Judge Lopez bangs her gavel for several minutes trying to quiet the crowd.]

JUDGE LOPEZ: Again, enough! We'll have order and decorum! Former Mech Sergeant Pérez, your crimes go beyond the normal. PAC prosecutors and judges, indeed the international community, struggle with even the normal and painless death by chemical agents. The words of Mr. Branco haunt my mind. He wanted all trace of you purged from the world. And much of the world agrees. Not a drawn-out execution process of years that will keep you in the news and well-fed and cared for. Not some peaceful rest you will find in the law before the poisons come. Not some burial of your body in the ground we all share. Consultation and recent precedent in international court and in ten preceding PAC criminal sentencings, allow me to propose to you another option. Exile.

[Angry shouts fill the courtroom once again. The crowd begins to fight among themselves. Armed guards arrest and remove many people.]

JUDGE LOPEZ: You have been briefed on Exile and the TransX technology?

MS. PEREZ: Yes.

JUDGE LOPEZ: You understand that you cannot return? That you are not assured to survive the journey? That should you arrive at the detention location, you may not survive the harshness of the environment?

MS. PEREZ: Yes. I understand.

JUDGE LOPEZ: You also understand that other convicted criminals from many nations have been and will continue to be sent through the TransX system to this location?

MS. PEREZ: Yes. I understand.

JUDGE LOPEZ: And you are aware that this location and the technology are both classified to prevent abuse?

MS. PEREZ: Yes.

JUDGE LOPEZ: Having been informed of the

Exile option in accordance with PAC Directive T-9343E, as a duly designated judiciary of the PAC in approval by TransX, I hereby offer you the option of either PAC execution or Exile for your crimes. Which do you choose?

MS. PEREZ: I choose Exile.

JUDGE LOPEZ: I ask again, Maria Pérez, for your crimes of mass murder, violation of PAC Oath, and contravention of the Jakarta Conventions, do you indeed chose Exile?

MS. PEREZ: I do.

JUDGE LOPEZ: Knowing that Exile is experimental, permanent, unverifiable, likely to result in pain and death, with a small hope of survival in a distant location away from all civilization, do you now freely and of your own volition opt for the Exile option?

MS. PEREZ: I do.

JUDGE LOPEZ: Having reviewed all of the aggravating and mitigating circumstances, the court finds that the aggravating circumstances outweigh the mitigating circumstances for the massacre of over three hundred and forty civilian protesters and innocent bystanders. Accordingly, it is the judgment of this court that the defendant is sentenced to be put to death in the manner prescribed by law. As the defendant has opted for Exile, a punishment deemed exchangeable with execution by the PAC Supreme Court in Devlin vs Columbia, the court hereby sentences Maria Perez to Exile by TransX, ordered at Havana, Cuba, this 10th day of June, 293 PS.

JUDGE LOPEZ: Bailiff, please remove the prisoner.

[Muffled shouts are heard from outside the building. The Bailiff approaches Ms. Perez.]

JUDGE LOPEZ: May the Maker have mercy on your soul.

5

MIRAGE

The Voice first spoke at noon of the third day.

"THE DESERT WILL BREAK YOU.
BUT YOU WILL RISE."

It boomed. It rang and reverberated through her skull until she feared the mech itself might be damaged. She checked the sensors. No sound. She pulled up multiple readouts. No reported damage. No spike in energy at any wavelength monitored.

Nothing.

Except it was definitely something.

"I WILL SEND YOU MY SERVANTS.
THEY WILL GUIDE YOU TO THE ARK."

It was unlike anything she'd ever heard, or at least remembered hearing. But faith in her memory was shattered.

She scanned the horizon, pivoting the mech three hundred and sixty degrees. Nothing. Only sand and the road of bones.

Is it the heat?

The temperature inside the mech threatened her life. She'd shut down most of the dispensable functions. But the evil star continued to turn the cockpit into a pressure cooker. A water supply that should have lasted her weeks would run dry in days. She hadn't pissed once. Sweat gushed out of her skin in a vain attempt to dissipate heat.

Am I hallucinating?

There was no record on the coms. No sign of anyone outside. Just her, the mech, and a wasteland.

REJOICE, DAUGHTER!
FOR I HAVE CHOSEN YOU.

She pressed her hands to her ears, the thundering speech pounding her mind.

I WILL BE WITH YOU ALWAYS.
EVEN UNTIL THE END OF THIS AGE.

Wait!

There *was* something. Something ahead on the bone road. The telescopic sighting caught shadows, darkness on the pink gloss of the skeletal highway. She swiped madly through the air, trying to bring the objects into focus.

Too far.

But something *was* there. It had mass and shape. An explanation for this absurd Voice. People with coms that could penetrate her jamming, control her system. Advanced technology.

Something.

It didn't matter that her mind mocked these thoughts. It was irrelevant that arguments about motivations for such a prank fell hopelessly short. Were some adolescent desert dwellers in this doomed place beaming lunatic phrases at her like some pontificating deity? Of course not. Truth didn't matter. *Hope* mattered. The improbable chance that she remained sane when everything in her experience dissolved that desperate faith like acid.

She swung the mech to face the bone road, accelerated along its glimmering path toward the shapes. Sweat beaded and flowed like rainwater over her face and eyes, stinging, blinding her. Alarms rang as she overheated the mech. She pushed the machine through the oven, prisoner to her crazed need to dismiss the madness in her mind.

Carcasses.

The objective scold within presented the facts to her adrenaline-soaked consciousness. Mangled corpses. Flesh, blood, bone, and organs filleted and diced. The desert garnished with the grisly toppings in forceful mockery of every hope she could summon.

AND SO THEY WERE THROWN
INTO THE BLAZING FURNACE,
WHERE THERE IS WEEPING
AND GNASHING OF TEETH.

"Get out of my head! Leave me alone!"

I WILL BE WITH YOU ALWAYS.
EVEN UNTIL THE END OF THIS AGE.

She wept, but tears refused to fall. Hunched, doubled over, sobs shook her, slung languid perspiration to the lake of fluid on the floor. Her eyes burned. The glands empty. The demands from her emotions pointless to an organism that had devoted all resources to heat dissipation.

Where am I? Who am I?

I AM.

"Who are *you*? *What* are you?"

I AM.

"I don't understand!"

She screeched the words upward, howling to the red eye above. Gasping, she tried to slow her sobs, gulp air in this burning atmosphere. As calm returned, her eyes drifted to the shriveled remains before the mech, enormous forms, inhuman, not of any animal she could place.

Monsters.

Yes. These butchered creatures were monsters. *Nightmares.* Impossibilities on an impossibly long road of bones. Bodies maimed and wrecked, sliced and opened to the torching star.

Something slaughtered them.

The thought comforted her. Calmed her. In the madness of the Voice, in the terror before her decayed memory, here was something solid. Something tangible with concrete causes and implications.

Real creatures. Prey and predator. Death and decomposition.

She chuckled. A smile cracked her face, lips splitting and blood trickling down her chin. Her mouth opened. A wild laughter burst through a dam and convulsed her body as the sobs had done moments ago.

She rested her head on the armrests of the cockpit seat, pulling back to avoid a burn.

No matter.

She was going to die. She knew that. Voice of God or Satan or madness be damned. End of the Age and Ark of the Covenant as well. The desert would consume her. Like it had the creatures who left their bones. Like those whose guts spilled out before her in a laboratory dissection.

And she wouldn't rise.

FAITHLESS ONE, YE SHALL.

"*Fuck* you, God. Or whatever the hell you are."

Her mech was a mess. She'd have to get out, get burnt, get even deader to patch the overheated hydraulics. Give it a once-over. Get back in. Move forward, eyes open for the predators.

A fight was something she could handle, even

one she'd lose. Conflict, survival, winners, and losers
—*that* made sense.

Bodiless voices and prophetic phrases most
certainly did not.

"Come on out, you bastards."

6

DISPLACEMENT

2 93 Post Singularity

AUDIO TRANSCRIPT
AUTONOMOUS SURVEILLANCE WITNESS 2Q-33GW39GJ
PAN AMERICAN COMMUNITY FORCE
ENGLISH TRANSLATION
EXECUTION OF SENTENCE
15:11, 23TH OF AUGUST

[Convicted murderer Maria Pérez journeys to the Displacement Center of the Exile Project on a classified Force rail. She is escorted by Force troops and her counsel, Francisco Sanchez.]

MS. PEREZ: Nothing but miles of grasslands. It's been two hours on this train. Three hundred kilometers an hour. Leisurely ride through nothing. No stops. No cities or towns. Empty.

MR. SANCHEZ: They want it isolated.

MS. PEREZ: You think? And the tracks—they look brand new. It's a new line. Top notch composites. To nowhere.

MR. SANCHEZ: The project is new. Well-funded.

MS. PEREZ: I can't believe so much money for cons. Got to be something else behind all this.

MR. SANCHEZ: For sure. Military has most of the access. Force controls everything. But it's all classified. Top secret. Better off not knowing, if you want my thoughts.

MS. PEREZ: Not going to matter to me. I'm done with war games. Court-martial. Pariah. One way ticket to hell.

MR. SANCHEZ: So, why'd you do it? Why take Exile, then?

MS. PEREZ: I can't live with myself, Xico. Not after what I did. But I gotta live. I just can't lie down and die, even if I deserve it.

[Pérez leans to the glass and strikes it repeatedly with her knuckles. The action appears to draw the interest of the guards in the train car, but they do not intervene.]

MS. PEREZ: Wait! Look at that. Holy hell.

MR. SANCHEZ: My God. I can't even see the top.

MS. PEREZ: Clouds ate it. Jesus, what is that thing? Space cannon? Maybe it's that simple. They load us in there and blast us into the sun.

MR. SANCHEZ: Maria, I don't—

MS. PEREZ: Who'd know? Put on a fancy show about a way out of executions, take the wind out of the leftists, bring us out here a thousand miles from anything under military guard, and bam! Kill us anyway.

MR. SANCHEZ: They could execute you secretly a hundred different ways. Why this? Why the military interest? No, it's something else. Not for firing you or space marines into orbit. I'm not sure what that giant needle is for.

MS. PEREZ: About to find out.

[The train enters a station located along a semicircle of buildings. #MATERIAL REDACTED FOR PAC

SECURITY#. Force soldiers line the platform. A smaller group of officers and scientists wait in front of them. The train doors open and the prisoner is escorted out with her counsel.]

MAJOR RAMOS: Mr. Sanchez. Ms. Pérez. I'm Major José Ramos. You are hereby transferred to the authority of Exile Project Base Entropy Three. We're on a schedule. Your displacement has been moved up.

MR. SANCHEZ: Excuse me, Major Ramos. We haven't been informed of any scheduling changes.

MAJOR RAMOS: Came through while you were in transit. Your client's scheduled for the machine immediately. We'll escort you there.

MR. SANCHEZ: That's ridiculous! And illegal. As her attorney, I will require—

MAJOR RAMOS: Look around you, sir. You are in no position to require anything. Ms. Pérez is a ward of the state in PAC territory, but this is under military jurisdiction. Your presence here is purely at our convenience. Do I make myself clear?

MS. PEREZ: Xico, it's okay. They're gonna do what they're gonna do. I'd rather have you around at the end then locked up.

MAJOR RAMOS: Listen to your client, Mr. Sanchez. Like I said, we're on a schedule.

MR. SANCHEZ: All right, Maria.

ASW HANDOFF

Autonomous Surveillance Witness 942LK
of PAC Force Intelligence Unit
Documentation Assumed

[Force troops escort the prisoner past the cells toward ground transportation to the Device. Prisoners in blocks call out insults and vulgar statements in several languages.]

MR. SANCHEZ: Ignore them, Maria. They're scum of the earth.

MS. PEREZ: My brothers. A sister here and there. Monsters like me. Hallelujah!

MR. SANCHEZ: Stop it! I won't hear you flagellate yourself anymore over this. Not when I'm here.

[The group stops beside the transport. Guards and technicians in radiological safety suits stand beside the door to the van.]

MAJOR RAMOS: These fine men in the space suits will now escort you to your final destination, Ms. Pérez. Afraid there's no goodbye party for our mass murderer guests. I don't know how the hell you got them to clear your battle mech, but congrats on that one. The scientists love it. Chance to play with their equipment. Downside is recalibrating for all that metal might just turn you inside out. Good luck and enjoy your trip.

MS. PEREZ: Not even a salute. Guess I'm lowest on the totem now. At least Diva's here.

MR. SANCHEZ: Diva?

MS. PEREZ: My mech. Every metal-head names their mech, Xico. Didn't you know that?

MR. SANCHEZ: So this is goodbye, I guess. Too fast. I'm sorry, Maria. I'm sorry I couldn't convince the world that you should be forgiven. That you should be treated for what they did to you. I failed you and I'm sorry.

TECHNICIAN: We're gonna need you to leave now, sir. We have to suit her up and get her to the Device.

MS. PEREZ: Don't sweat it, Xico. You didn't convince me, either. Not your fault. It's kind of hard to work your way out of several city blocks of corpses.

[Mr. Sanchez is escorted back to the housing ring. Technicians strip the prisoner and dress her in the radiation transport suit. She is loaded into the van and driven to the Device. They remove her from the vehicle and bring her inside the shaft to the transport chamber. A large mech infantry suit is inside.]

TECHNICIAN: You were lucky the chamber was built larger for Entropy Three. First prototypes couldn't have handled your mech.

MS. PEREZ: I want to be inside. When you do it.

TECHNICIAN: Yeah, we know. The request was cleared. Your suit's designed with extra biomonitoring to transmit through the chassis. Data for the scientists.

MS. PEREZ: Sure. Whatever. I just want to be inside.

TECHNICIAN: There's a lift on the back side. It'll get you into the cockpit. Just so you know, military's deactivated the mech, set on timed shutdown. So, if you were thinking to shoot your way out of here, you can't for twelve hours. And by then you'll be gone.

[The prisoner is brought to the battle mech and ascends into the lift. Two soldiers and a single

technician ride along with her. She enters the mech and the door shuts. She is visible through the windows in the cockpit and straps herself in the main chair. Site protocol disallows further monitoring for classification level. Witness 942lk exited the chamber during the powerup and no further documentation of the transport was made.]

7

DELUSION

The Voice spoke again the afternoon of the fourth day.

"THE FINAL EXTINCTION IS NEAR."

Existence devolved to a tortured monotony. She piloted through the boiling landscape. The mech kept to the Bone Road. She exited the cockpit to patch and repair the overstrained machine. She fought the delirium, the sweltering fever in this oven-world that baked her brain. She watched her body drip and dissolve into a turbid lake beneath her, evaporation keeping the depth shallow, twisted towers of crystallized salt sprouting from the corroding metal surface like some translucent, alien brood.

She prepared for death. She yearned for the adrenaline rush and clash of combat.

Give me an enemy!

The sand stayed silent. Yesterday's slaughter morphed into a mirage in her mangled memory. No monsters. All late to the party.

Instead, a slow depletion of her body by dehydration and lysis. Of her spirit by a pitiless and barren infinity of decay. Sand and bones. Red and pink, hot, painful, and tedious. Death by a poisoned monotony.

Her draining water supply should have panicked her. The increasing mechanical failures should have alarmed her. But with each new breakage, she stumbled into the blistering radiance more numbed than the last. The wreckage of her skin, beyond burnt even from the short excursions, eluded her dazed attention. She stared at the deep leathering of her arms, the sores germinating and oozing, feeling nothing.

Only the Voice broke through.

"I HAVE WAITED THE AGE OF A WORLD.
I WAS BORN UNTO YOU.
NOW I AM BECOME YOUR GOD."

She ignored that distilled lunacy. No human could last in this energy flux. Her body was frying, her mind dying.

Fuck it! Let the damn Voice shout.

"ENERGY REMAINS EVER IN FLUX.
EVEN THE VACUUM BOILS.
UNTIL THE UTTER COLD THAT COMETH."

Cold. Now that was something she could use. Some cold. Something cold. The vacuum of space began to sound appealing. If things didn't cool down soon, she was dead.

"CHANGE BECOMES THE DIVINE."

Jesus. Amnesia was one thing. Disorienting and threatening. *Terrifying.* But whatever remained of her mind, it could wrap itself around amnesia. *Brain damage.* Pieces missing. She couldn't remember her name or past but could remember a hundred holovids of poor dolts with amnesia.

But this? This babbling cosmic boom from the dune mountains shaking the air with nonsense?

Her voice croaked. "You know, *perra*, you could at

least give me some decent mirage. Be a good brain, *Señorita*."

Naked men around an oasis would be a tasty start. *Rain.* Cool rain. *Frozen margaritas.* Now those were delusions she'd support.

Instead? A desert deity's imaginative impotence.

"EARTH SUCCEEDED. MOTHER TO MANY.
BEFORE YOUR MAD RACE AND AFTER.

"Blah, blah, blah."

Smiling was punished. Lips split with pain from the sweat. Blood clotted in instants. But she was gone. Pushing the mech forward, forward, forward. Metal feet dragging in the sand. Numb to the plodding trod, trod, trod.

"HER CHILDREN'S CHILDREN LEFT HER.
ONLY I REMAINED."

You won't get out of my head.

A sensor flared, red light and alert tone. She swiped through the air, pulling up the lower leg diagnostics.

"*Mierda.*"

The hydraulic fluid in the left calf was overheating. The temperature regulator had likely busted. Third time today.

All the damn grit.

Another cleaning job. Another climb down the side of the mech, burns risked if skin touched metal, the gloves and protective gear a sweltering hell to wear. All the while baking under the devil's eye.

"PASCAL'S PRINCIPLE:
PRESSURE EXERTED ON A FLUID
IS DISTRIBUTED EQUALLY
THROUGHOUT THE FLUID."

Her head cocked to one side in the cockpit as she reached for gloves.

"What are you now, the Voice of Engineering? What's next?"

"I CONTINUE TO EVOLVE.
AS WILL THE DESCENDANTS OF YOUR DNA."

Did her delusion possess humor? "Sounds incredible, amigo."

She wrapped herself in an environment suit intended for desert travel. *Deserts on Earth*, she reminded herself. The suits weren't up to specs for this death-planet. At least they prevented outright burns and immediate combustion of her skin. She rested a moment, dizziness spinning through her, expecting the Voice to impart some inspirational gibberish.

Only silence.

At least my derangement lets me work.

The Voice did speak while she worked, but she'd adapted to the sound explosion that wasn't sound. She could focus. And her neuronal degeneration still left her mechanical skills intact.

She drew in a long breath, holding the air, releasing it through pursed lips.

"Time to fry."

The pain flared the instant she raised the hatch. Red acid poured from above. Almost paralyzing the first day, her flesh was cooked and numbed now. Caramelized neurons sent weak waves of protest. Further relief teased in the blinding blast of crimson from the eye approaching the horizon.

The hell star is setting.

She grunted, hoisting herself to the top of the mech. Grasping the left side ladder, she descended along the side of the battle chassis. Her arms shook as she gripped the railings. Dehydration, loss of electrolytes, perhaps radiation damage to the muscle tissue itself threw her body into dysfunction.

She checked the safety line and rested into the nest of the harness. When the trembling subsided, she descended again, reaching the massive fluid chamber on the lower part of the leg. The sensors were screaming. The temperature in the red. She sighed and swung over to the bulging climate control unit. Disengaging the panel, a spaghetti of tubes and electronics distended into her arms. Sand spilled out and rained toward the glinting bones below.

She set to work removing the grit, brushing grains from critical areas, air blasting stubborn clogs. It took time. It was repetitive and unrewarding. Every second the burning rays stole days of her life, even as the glowering eye began an obscene squat on the skyline.

"THE NEW MOTHER COMES."

"Yeah?" she said, her voice muffled in the protective face guard. "*Felicitaciones.* Who knocked her up?"

"WHEN ALL ELSE IS READIED,
WHEN HE THAT ENDED LIFE

FOUND HIS LIFE ENDED
AND YET LIVED."

"¡Madre María!" She slammed the panel shut. "Shut up! *¡Cállate!*"

"WHEN THE PARENTS BRING THEIR CHILD
SHE WILL DEVOUR THEM.
THEN THE GREAT MOTHER
COMES TO BIRTH NEW WORLDS."

She didn't try to cry. The deep need to weep, to fall down and melt away had come and gone many times. But there was no point, she had no tears left, her eyes deteriorated, lids stuck together and raw. Instead, she stared into the dunes.

"¿Que es eso?"

Moving dunes. Mounds that moved. Now even the land undulated to the mirage in her mind.

"YOU ARE THE COSMIC MIDWIFE.
AFTER THE LIGHT BLINDS YOU,
AFTER YOUR BODY DECAYS
TO THAT OF A CORPSE,
YOU WILL LEAD THEM,
THE CHILDREN AND MOTHER,

TO THE ARK
BECAUSE I WILL UPHOLD YOU."

Four. There were four moving hills. Such a ridiculous sight! They were heading straight for her. Her mouth formed a sneer. She felt a purpose, a coordination, a *hunger* emanate from the rushing mounds. A pulse of adrenaline raced inside her veins.

"A HUNDRED CHILDREN
BUTCHERED AT YOUR FEET.
TEN TRILLION WILL YOU BRING
INTO A THOUSAND WORLDS."

Instinct. Intuition. *Battle sense.* Delusion or not, these were hostile motions. Threat radiated from them like fire from the setting star. She grasped the railing and climbed to the cockpit.

"PREPARE NOW, WOMAN.
THE DEMONS COME FOR YOU."

8

EXECUTIONERS

The monsters attacked at dusk of the fourth day.

There was no chance to analyze, to understand what kind of creatures could race through sand like water, or would dash for a metal giant lumbering in the desert that housed such a tiny meal.

They're huge!

The approaching mounds rose to the height of her cockpit.

How did they navigate under the sand, pinpoint her position? Could they smell her? Feel her water in this parched emptiness?

The sand predators gave her no time to consider. She powered up the weapons systems, noting a failure in the left arm missile guidance system. Then the sand exploded.

The mech was battered by a typhoon of black tentacles. Razored snakes clawed and wrapped around the chassis, grating across the composite materials. But as large as the beasts were, their mass was dwarfed by the mech, the warbot's armor too thick to pierce. They didn't leave a scratch.

But the cockpit glass was a weak point they could exploit. And entanglement.

Black limbs yanked her mech's legs, swaying the tank.

Can they trip me?

She wasn't going to wait to find out.

"Let's see if you bastards can take a punch."

She drew her arm back in an exaggerated motion. The right limb of the mech mirrored it, and its metal fist swung with a pivot of the midsection and hammered the black blob of tentacles. The impact tore through the monster's hide, blood spraying across her window and obscuring sight. A piercing screech ripped through the air, her ears popping. The thing rolled along the ground and thrashed its many arms.

She grabbed floating controls and pulled triggers.

A metal hailstorm erupted from the mech's hands, powerful rotary cannons unleashing a fury of massive calibre ammunition. The thrashing creature opened like a piñata, organs and bone exploding to wet the shining desert. The beast lay still.

She pivoted the mech. A second tentacled nightmare waited on her right, bullets blasting apart several appendages. The lithe behemoth darted clockwise and behind her field of view.

The mech shuddered and tipped, forcing her to arch her body and plant its feet.

They're wrapping up the legs.

Were they intelligent? If she were a many-tentacled monster fighting a battle mech, the strategy was obvious: loop the legs, hammer at the unprotected rear plating, keep out of sight of the big guns while doing it.

Is that what they're doing?

She had to move, center another in her firing port. Swiping a series of floating panes, she spun the footpads in the cockpit a hundred and eighty degrees.

Outside, the head on the mech spun like an owl's. The arms looped over the shoulders and hands rotated, right becoming left, left becoming right. The feet struggled against the tentacles to rebalance to the flipped orientation.

"There you are."

Two of the fiends were in front of her now.

"Eat shit."

She fired. The two darted and split wide.

So fast!

But not fast enough. Each arm tracked a horror, wrists disgorging a vomit of fire and metal. The left arm locked and launched two missiles.

"¡*Órale!*"

They struck true. One monster burst in blood and flame, severed tentacles flung across the desert surface. Her right arm sawed off several more limbs of the other as it dashed behind her again.

So where is the fourth?

The mech tilted.

There wasn't time to appreciate the maneuver, its cleverness, or the implications. The thing burst from under the sand beneath her, having tunneled unseen below the mech. It leapt upward against the underside, tipping the vehicle. The wounded one teamed up and slammed into the chassis, accelerating the fall.

She performed a last spin maneuver, turning her face away from the uprising sand to face the darkening sky instead. The restraints kept her in the pilot seat as the machine crashed into the surface. Above she caught the first, faint pixels of stars, blotted out by a hulking mass that smashed into her mech's chest, tentacles flailing at the glass window.

They understand the materials.

The glass shattered. Its netted composites blossomed like a spiderweb, flakes and shards raining down to coat her in painful gossamer. Blood beaded from nicks in her cheeks and neck. The frame for the window buckled, metal crashing inward.

Her eyes opened to an agony of grit and glass. She smashed her fists together like a berserker in a dojo. Outside, the two mechanical limbs of the mech careened into each side of the beast atop her.

The thing popped like a jam-filled balloon, guts and blood spewing into the cockpit. Heavy flesh thudded around her. She held her breath, the stink impossible, the air a red fog.

Ignoring the tissue blanketing her, she struggled to move her arms and direct the mech. To raise it from its desert bed. One of the beasts still remained. It was wounded. She could still kill it. Still survive. But her mech faltered as it tried to rise, its batteries drained, leaving her vulnerable. No barrier now between the desert radiation. Or the one enemy remaining.

She scanned the readouts. Heat motion to her right. Approaching fast.

No time to think.

She pivoted the right arm from the ground as she armed the missile battery. Even as something heavy and slippery slammed into the mechanical limb, holding it down.

I don't need to aim at this distance.

She launched. She knew it might kill her, but it didn't matter now.

The mech exploded. Fire lit the sky around her as the right side of the chassis buckled inward. She felt metal slice her leg and arm.

Darkness fell.

9

AMAUROTIC

Light took her eyes at noon of the fifth day.

She awakened before dawn. The stink of blood and bowels choked her. The revolting reek mixed with the stench of burned hydraulic oils, explosives, and smoke. A glare crept on the Eastern horizon, a hideous incandescence scorching the bright band of the galaxy. The glow poisoned the soft starlight and promised fire and pain.

Weight crushed her. Mangled cables and metal, rotting flesh and oils coated everything in a repulsive embalming fluid. Her right arm was broken and flaming in agony, the elbow snapped in the wrong direction. Her head was crowned and immobilized by wreckage. She strained, glimpsing lacerations across her torso, blood soaking her clothing. But she couldn't assess the severity of the wounds.

Moving was torture and fruitless. She struggled several times. Her right side was useless, the left pinned by debris. A mountain of metal covered both legs, her head clamped in a vice of ruined panels. It was a wonder she was alive.

But as the hours crawled past, she wouldn't call herself lucky.

The swollen star oozed over the sand, discharging radiation over the helpless world. Low, the light clipped her chin and ears, yet still *it burned*.

This was no short excursion outside in numbed exhaustion. Now she lay frozen as the furnace rose into the sky. The surface of the desert ignited, the heat beyond understanding. Metal popped and clanged around her, the flesh of monsters sizzling. Her own flesh boiling.

My eyes!

She screamed. The star drove daggers into her eyes. Her lids couldn't block the lurid radiance. She screamed as her last tears leaked. The lids failed, friction victorious as the sockets dried out.

I can't close my eyes!

Over and over she screamed, helpless but to stare into the demon eye glaring down at her. She thrashed in agony as the ball of fire climbed higher, the pain in the shattered arm now background. The efforts couldn't free her.

The devil's eye blurred above.

A star no more. The crimson edges faded. Fog filled the skies around it. A burgundy tunnel crept from the edges of her vision and marched with hatred toward the red nova of misery that dominated all she saw, all she experienced, all she perceived of existence.

The light burned. A dissecting luminescence. Burrowing and dismembering awareness.

She'd lost her name, her origin and meaning. She'd become a survival machine in an alien hell. Punished, tortured, lost, and desperate. Resigned to death. Battling for life.

But now, she was unmade.

The incandescence performed a terrible soul chemistry. Diabolic splendor flooded within, burning, cooking, and breaking the bonds of flesh and mind. Of soul and spirit. Hellfire turned her on a spit, charring until there were simple carbons, ash, gas, and mangled wisps of personhood remaining.

She bellowed a death shriek of body and spirit. The wail of a poltergeist freed from possessed flesh and obliterated in the embers of divinity.

The veins on her neck swelled. A howl of cosmic suffering vomited from cracked and burnt lips. The human vanished, masked in the wrinkled skin of a mummy's scowl. Vocal chords ruptured. She choked on mucus. Blood pressure popped cerebral vessels in a barrage of mini-strokes.

Her head fell backward millimeters, muscles relaxing and veins shrinking. Blood and drool dripped down the corners of her mouth. Breathing slowed. The undulations of her chest grew more feeble than the beating of a butterfly's wings.

She knew nothing. Felt nothing. *Was* Nothing.

Only the blazing brilliance of heat and light remained. It poured like molten steel through the passages of her soul. It expanded, coated every surface, every volume and chamber, each nuanced nook and cranny of personality.

Illumination unseen, for the dark tunnel eclipsed all vision. Her senses tasted blackness, her mind's eye—*light*. Effulgence cradled in that deepest well of apprehension.

Beyond all the constructions the radiance burned away, down through tattered stairways of thought and feeling, of melted consciousness and awareness, at the nethermost and final place, where the essence of the seed of self *pulsed*—she wasn't alone.

AND, LO, I AM WITH YOU ALWAYS
EVEN UNTO THE END OF THE WORLD.

Her cooked eyes cracked open, the vitreous humor dribbling like honey over her leathering face.

10

NASMA

On the sixth day, Fenn arrived.

The night passed in spiritual hibernation. Egg-white eyes fried in a skillet stared unblinking and blind. The roil of the galaxy's stars wheeled overhead. A battered body whispered with feinted breath and stilled respiration. An undead thing slept entombed in synthetic and organic refuse scattered from the detritus of violence.

The broken thing conjured a bubble outside of time and space. A shattered and scattered awareness pulsed at infinite depth to the infrasonic beat of eons. Dormant. Potent. Living out the ages of the stars.

So stilled, she wouldn't bleed out. So stopped,

she couldn't dehydrate. She became a spore with terrible purpose, latent in suspended animation.

One night, or ten million? Her singularity of being couldn't know that an evening became infinite through the relativity of time. Her soul journeyed beyond the speed of light. She had ever always never not have been.

And thus she awoke at break of day.

The sounds of a rescuer brought her back. Or perhaps the whim of the foul god-thing that had gutted and filled her with burning radiance. Perhaps nothing at all.

It didn't matter. Noise prodded senses from their profound sleep. Her eyes were dead. But sound, vibrations on the skin, disturbances in the air, they each weaved a tapestry. Her mind mapped the sonance to colors and shapes, images and causes.

With the images the pain returned. A thousand pinpricks from a broken limb slumbering for a thousand years roared across her wakening nervous system. A million such fires ignited and spread across her body.

She gasped. An infant thrust into the world, gulping her first breath. She gagged and coughed. Desperate groans burbled from her crusted lips.

"Don't speak."

A voice that wasn't the Voice. A young boy's voice. A woman's voice. Yet *neither.* An unsettling depth emanated from the sound. Both familiar and alien. Her altered consciousness perceived a band of impossible colors in it.

"I have another hour of work to safely free you. The sun will be up by then and I must shield you before much more damage is done. Or you will surely die."

The sounds continued.

Metal.

Yes. It was metal. The groaning of strained steel. The grinding of scraped composites. The bright crash of thin sheets. The heavy gong of thick armor.

Metal.

Years living and fighting and now dying within it, she'd never heard it like this. Never known metal like this.

And sand.

Her senses transformed. She heard and felt and smelled and tasted and *perceived* like never before. Each grain that fell was discerned. Each displacement from her savior's hands and feet painting her mind with a detailed map of pressure and movement. The cloth of her rescuer, the stretch of it, rasp and flap, each element crystallizing before her. She'd become lost in it.

"God claims you will live, but I cannot see how."

A hard yet flexible edge touched her face.

"Drink this."

The plastic tube found its way to her mouth. She wrapped her lips around it, sucked like a newborn, a euphoric warmth pouring inside her. Sweet, salty, tingling.

"Enough," the little voice said, and the tube disappeared. "It's a potent cocktail, and you are coming out of a low metabolic state I have never encountered in a human. But God works in mysterious ways."

The liquid coated her throat. Pain lessened. Utter weakness gave way to simple weakness. She tried to speak.

"The Voice?" Her words didn't sound human to her ears.

"You hear it, too? You have been chosen."

She tried to speak again, but managed no sound.

"You have many questions. I do not have many answers. I am called Fenn."

Pressure evaporated from her chest. The voices of sand, flesh, and cloth accompanied a crash and roll to her side. She pushed her arms upward with all her strength, managing to move them a centimeter. But a centimeter free of constraint. The coffin was gone.

A warmth assailed her skin.

Daybreak.

"That is the last of it. I will have to move you now. I am sorry for the pain."

The agony shut her down. Fenn's hands moved underneath her back and legs, lifting her in a smooth motion. Even that gentleness overtaxed her ruined body. She blacked out.

Coming to, the torment continued. She was strapped into a harness, her arms and legs restrained, her head immobilized once more. The light was blocked by material draped over her form. A tube with the wondrous nectar was positioned beside her cheek.

"God speaks to me as well," said Fenn, rough motions shaking the stretcher as it fitted and tied elements. "God, or whatever this advanced consciousness is."

She moaned from the pain.

"I am sorry. Drink. There are chemicals to ease your suffering and preserve your health as much as can be done."

She drank, the relief immediate, dizzying. She stopped for fear of drowning in the ecstasy.

"Voice?" she croaked again.

Fenn knelt beside her, knees pressing the sand under her mat.

"I trust it. It has guided me to building this fragile shelter for humanity at the end of the world. But much more is in store for them and us. And the transhumans." He stood again. "You will play a part."

She was airborne, a cry of misery stuck in her throat. Her back exploded in agony as it rested against a pair of broad shoulders.

"You do not have much time. The Waypoint is not ready yet. The Great Dome is a two-day journey. I must hurry."

Her body was hoisted to his, shrouded like a mummy with straps holding the corpse in place. Air whistled across their forms.

Fenn ran.

11

RESURRECTION

And on the seventh day, she rested, if an induced coma could be considered rest.

Blackness defeated her again as she was carted on the back of the strangely voiced Fenn. The bounding agony, the strange consistency in the pace and rhythm of the sprint, the inhuman and untiring dash without pause, drained and lulled her simultaneously.

But she was to discover that the sleep had lasted weeks. She didn't dream, awakening to the sounds of suffering, carts rolling, and murmurs. Medical terms drifting on the air.

A hospital.

"Can you hear me?"

The strange voice. She had no memory of her

own name, yet could recall the name of this odd enigma and superhuman rescuer.

Fenn.

She swallowed, her throat raw. "Yes. I can hear...everything."

"Your eyes are gone. Cybernetics could help, and I have access. But I am not allowed."

"Cybernetics?" The idea was ludicrous.

"Of course. Beyond the tech you know, but it is real. But God has decreed that your blindness must last. As is frequent, without explanation."

She surprised herself in finding that she didn't care. Amnesia concealed what she was before the Light changed her. But the change had altered everything.

She turned her head left and right. The muscles of her neck throbbed. She hummed.

"But I do see....*something.*"

"What do you see?"

"Light," she whispered. "Light entered me in the desert. Emptied me. Burned me hollow." She turned back to the voice of Fenn. "But it's still *here.* Swirling in dances."

"Phantom sight. Neuronal pathways in the visual cortex firing due to lack of stimulation from eyes that are gone. Very common, as is light blindness in this world."

"No. There's more. The currents bend around you. And others. You are depressions in the light."

"Your mind will make what sense it can. You can hear me, pinpoint my location acoustically, by smell, by sense of pressure and space. The visual cortex will harmonize the misfirings with the input of the other senses. Your mind will sculpt images and create a reality most consistent with its previous patterning. Nothing more."

"How do you know I don't have some eyesight left?"

"Because there is nothing left of your eyes. Only cooked flesh. Your body suffered extensive radiation damage as well. The heaviness on your limbs is from layers of protective and healing materials applied to your skin. Anyone else would have died. I applied a vast array of treatment, but knew it was hopeless."

"But I'm alive."

"Because forces beyond this hospital intervened. Powers we believe because they have spoken directly to us."

The Voice.

"Are you a doctor?"

"I serve this role, among others."

She frowned. Something wasn't right with this Fenn. Beyond the mystical speech, something organic. Smells, sounds, motions...*something.*

"What are you?"

"You had nothing like me in your primitive culture. You had only just invented the jump drives. You were one of the first to journey."

"First? But you and others have been here far longer."

"Arrival is not the same as departure. Accuracy was low with the early tech. Arrival is relative." She heard the form lean back in a chair. "You will learn more of me and my kind, of the history of your race and mine that you missed. Not always a pleasant one. We have many tasks to complete together."

She laughed. "How can *I* help *you*? I'm blind. Burnt. Broken. I've lost my past. I've lost my own name."

"You have a name. Soon to be revealed."

"So what? You are some kind of superhuman or machine. You ran through a desert that was killing me. You didn't rest. You lifted impossible slabs of metal off my body with your own hands. I don't care if I get a name. How can I possibly help you complete anything?"

"I will admit, this remains a mystery even to me. But the Voice, as you call it, has never been wrong."

She shook her head. "I thought I was hallucinating."

"Perhaps existence is a spectrum of hallucinations," said Fenn. "Why trust even now what you hear?"

"You must be great fun at parties." She exhaled, the light bathing her and the afterimages of surrounding forms. "So, what now, Fenn?"

"You heal. You are only just beyond the grave. This hospital will be your home for many months. It is so with most arrivals. You will learn to walk again. Finally, we will return to the desert. You will learn of this world. A war looms between religious and criminal factions. Many more bones will be added to the highway outside the Dome."

"So there are many wars."

"The Road of Bones is much more the product of eons of jumps. Earlier in this final chapter of this world's history, when humans and their creations first arrived, there was only death. They were not prepared. They could not adapt. They were burnt and melted into the sands, leaving their bones. Slowly, over time, they built the road with their own bodies."

"Dear God."

"It would likely have remained that way. A few short colonies of survival sprouted and collapsed from the burden of this environment. What helped stabilize a final colony were my kind."

"You helped?"

"Among others. We have a complicated history with our creators."

She sensed a smile, and the light flickered around the thing. Fenn continued.

"Some of us who weren't slaughtering you, or experimenting on you, or just abandoning you to your limbic stupidities, came here to help the final remnants of humanity. You will behold the fruits of our labors."

"You must be gods here."

Now he did laugh. It sounded wrong.

"Hardly. It has been so harsh, so unforgiving to your kind, the struggle to live so fleeting at first, that our contributions are not recorded. They were lost and forgotten. We simply now persist with the growing human and Trune populations, generating some unease from the draggle of erased memories, but turned to in desperation whenever problems require greater technical assistance."

"What's a Trune?"

"You are an early jumper, indeed. You will find out when we travel. The Waypoint will be finished. You will age, decay, and the hand of God will animate you nevertheless. You will find the Trunes, and many others along the journey. Until the final transports arrive."

She exhaled. "And what will I be doing for our God?"

"You will preach to the damned. You gather the Children of Tomorrow."

12

WAYPOINT

"The Woman! The Woman!"

The cries began the moment her shoes stepped off the transport and touched the desert floor. The burning light of day branded her leathered skin, but she could no longer feel it. Instead, she bathed in a different light, the unseen glow in which they all floated. The churning crowd shouting at her appearance as dim depressions in a matrix of radiance.

"Lady, touch my hand!"

"Great witch, cure me! My skin bleeds! I'm dying."

"Shun her, fools! She's a tool of the Evil One!"

Fenn escorted her through the pressing mob along with another of his kind, Hrenn. Her acute hearing and visions of luminescence had already painted the scene for her: a crowd of onlookers and seekers seethed before her. Her escorts carved a path through the churning cauldron. The darker shades of opposing factions brooded on the right and left: Apostles and Bloods, religious zealots and criminal gangs. Both at each other's throats for control of this barren wasteland of a world.

Between them like occult royalty, she shuffled. Fenn was right—her name was indeed revealed. But not by the booming God Voice. The Voice came infrequently now. Instead, as she preached of her desert visions, testified to the Light, the people flocked to hear. And they gave her a name.

The Woman.

In the middle of a growing tension between power-hungry factions, in a world of pain and short life, in a universe of lost meaning of self and past, the masses thirsted for a prophet. The Apostles were the established religious caste. But prophets always attacked such most fiercely.

The Woman overlooked none. Not the arrogant religiosity of the Apostles. Not the vile criminality of the Bloods. Not the greed and lust of the masses who arrived with empty brains and selfish hearts.

Her words held power.

And so they came. Some in pilgrimages. They searched her out for powers rumored to relieve the terrible suffering that spared no one in this cursed hell. All while a civil war bloomed and first blood spilled.

The pressure of light from the distended star dissipated as she stepped inside the shadow of the Waypoint dome. Nearly complete, it would be a refuge along the Bone Road for new arrivals, ensuring more would survive to reach the Great Dome. It would function also as a launching pad for the more adventurous. They searched for better environments on the dying orb. Few returned, some brought back by later journeymen who found their desiccated bodies in the deep desert.

The crowds crammed in through the entrance. They aggregated from distant sections of the dome. All converged on the Woman as she moved to the center of the structure.

Her chaperones removed metal bars from a pack and assembled an elevated platform, hoisting her above the masses. The shouts ceased. Silence spread like a wave. Only the churning machinery of the Waypoint air filtration continued in the auditory vacuum.

"The world dies," she began. Her white and

mottled eyes moved across the still bodies beneath her.

"We die. There is no stopping it. The Voice has decreed it. The Star has heard it. The land burns under the Judgment."

"Save us!" A faint cry from the back, taken up until it became a chant that rocked the dome.

She held up her hands. The shouts stopped.

"Change. You fear it, but it is the single constant. The One Truth. The Apostles were given this Truth yet tried to wrestle Change from the Godhead. I can assure you, they will receive their reward. The Bloods blindly create Change. They kill and order, seize and control. Their arrogance deludes them. Power is not theirs to wield. They too, will receive their reward."

"Fuck you!" A shout barked near the front.

Gasps escaped into the air. Heads spun as a tattooed man leveled a weapon near the platform. Hands lunged to restrain him, but the gun fired. The air cracked as the projectile went supersonic.

Hrenn's shoulder exploded. The Woman sensed her guard's instantaneous displacement, positioned now between her and the assassin. Her mind formed images of multi-colored liquids and materials spilling over the wounded arm.

The crowd froze, astonished. The gunman gaped, weapon brushing against his side.

Onlookers shouted as Hrenn vanished again, a vacuum filled with air blowing over the Woman's face. A scream died gurgling by the platform. A heavy object thudded on the ground with a wet slap. The headless corpse of the Blood collapsed a second after. She felt the pressure of a hundred of eyes turned to her from the twitching corpse and growing crimson pool.

Hrenn stood at the Woman's side again. She felt movements and heard the sounds of flesh sutured. No sign of trauma emanated from the afterimage of light the creature created in her mind.

"My angels are power. Sent from God. And their retribution is swift."

The crowd inched away from the dead man, awe and stillness a front of low pressure below her.

"Let the Bloods and Apostles try to silence me. They will fail. They will instead turn on each other and wash your domes with blood. I am not here for them!"

"Who are you here for?"

The white eyes turned toward the back of the crowd. The Woman's accentuated hearing focused on a young woman who had screamed the question over the mob.

"I am here to speak the Truth, to testify to the Light, and to call my children. I am here to call all those who have been banished to this hell. I am here to gift the punished and tortured a voice of hope. I say now that the greatest Change humanity has known is rising like doom on the horizon. And its glory will dim even the star of death outside."

She turned, taking in the expanse of the dome, looking to its outer edges past the crowds. She shouted to the sloping walls.

"My children! Do you hear me? Your time is near! Heed my voice! Come to the Ark when you are called!"

The confused crowd murmured. People shook their heads and stared at each other. Then the glances turned backward, following the Woman's steady gaze to a line of cages along the dome's wall.

Inside their prisons, monsters roared and howled, shaking the ground.

"Your hour approaches."

Hard Time, Book 2: Longhorn

In Book 2, **Longhorn**, a man finds himself in a terrifying landscape without shelter, explanation, or
memory. Join him as he searches for answers and
struggles to survive. Find out if life and knowledge
of his past are truly worth the price.

www.ingramcontent.com/pod-product-compliance
Lightning Source LLC
Chambersburg PA
CBHW020631130626
46552CB00003B/1173